P9-DEL-369

Dear Parents,

Welcome to the Scholastic Reader series. We have taken over 80 years of experience with teachers, parents, and children and put it into a program that is designed to match your child's interests and skills.

Level 1—Short sentences and stories made up of words kids can sound out using their phonics skills and words that are important to remember.

Level 2—Longer sentences and stories with words kids need to know and new "big" words that they will want to know.

Level 3—From sentences to paragraphs to longer stories, these books have large "chunks" of texts and are made up of a rich vocabulary.

Level 4—First chapter books with more words and fewer pictures.

It is important that children learn to read well enough to succeed in school and beyond. Here are ideas for reading this book with your child:

- Look at the book together. Encourage your child to read the title and make a prediction about the story.
- Read the book together. Encourage your child to sound out words when appropriate. When your child struggles, you can help by providing the word.
- Encourage your child to retell the story. This is a great way to check for comprehension.
- Have your child take the fluency test on the last page to check progress.

Scholastic Readers are designed to support your child's efforts to learn how to read at every age and every stage. Enjoy helping your child learn to read and love to read.

—**Francie Alexander**
Chief Education Officer
Scholastic Education

To Rachel, with love,
—Aunt Gracie

For Debbie, Chris, and Chris,
who keep good time
—M.H.

Library of Congress Cataloging-in-Publication Data is available.

ISBN: 0-590-30859-9

10 9 8 7 6 5 05 06 07
Printed in the U.S.A. 23 • First printing, September 1997

MONSTER MATH

School Time

by **Grace Maccarone**

Illustrated by **Marge Hartelius**

Math Activities by **Marilyn Burns**

Scholastic Reader — Level 1

SCHOLASTIC INC. Cartwheel BOOKS®

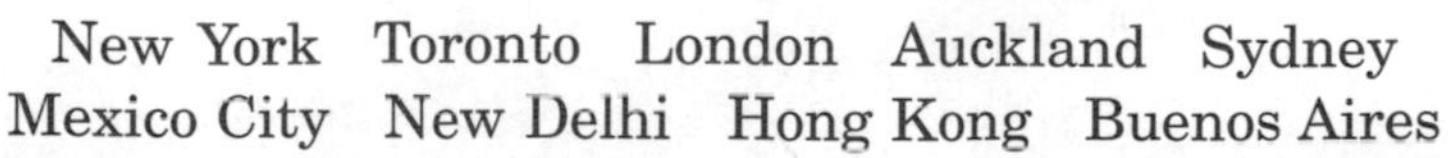

New York Toronto London Auckland Sydney
Mexico City New Delhi Hong Kong Buenos Aires

12 1 2 3 4 5 6 7 8 9 10 11

At six o'clock, monsters wake.

MONSTER
cooking
OIL

At seven o'clock,
they make a mistake.

At eight o'clock,
they go to school.

Then monsters learn
a safety rule.

At nine o'clock,
monsters spell.

At ten o'clock,
they show and tell.

At eleven o'clock,

monsters read.

Then each monster
plants a seed.

Monster Specials
Monster Mush
Monster Meat Balls
Monster Mud Pies

At twelve o'clock,

monsters eat.

GO, MON

At one o'clock,
they compete.

At two o'clock,
they subtract.

Then monsters learn
a science fact.

At three o'clock,

monsters go.

At four o'clock,
they catch and throw.

At five o'clock,
they paste and glue.

Then monsters eat
a yummy stew.

At six o'clock,
they take a bath.

At seven o'clock,
they play monster math.

At eight o'clock,
they shut the light.

Monsters are asleep.
Good night!

• About the Activities •

Children often see people looking at clocks or referring to their watches. "It's 3:30. We need to leave for the movies." "Grandma will be here soon; it's almost 5 o'clock." "You can stay up tonight until 8:30."

Children are familiar with people telling time from clocks and watches, but learning how to tell time by themselves is a complicated process. They need to learn about analog clocks and watches, with two hands or three and with different kinds of numerals. They need to learn about digital clocks and watches. And they need many opportunities for connecting times on all types of timekeepers to their daily routines.

Although it takes some children longer than others to learn to tell time, all children do it eventually. Read the story with your child. If your child seems interested in learning how to tell time, then use the activities to get your child started.

You and your child will also find the Hello Math Reader *Just a Minute* useful and enjoyable for talking about time. The book and activities focus on learning about a specific measure of time — one minute.

— Marilyn Burns

You'll find tips and suggestions
for guiding the activities whenever
you see a box like this!

Retelling the Story

Read the story again. After you read each page, look at the two clocks in the illustration. Point to each and say what time it shows. (If you need help telling the times, try saying the times along with an adult or an older child.)

What clues on each clock help you tell what time it is?

Now read the story again and try telling the time on the clocks. What are you usually doing at that time?

Note that on four pages, the times are not on the hour. These clocks show 8:15, 11:30, 2:30, and 5:30. Unless your child is particularly motivated, it's not necessary to explain the intricacies of telling these times. Just talk about them as being after 8 o'clock (or 11, 2, or 5 o'clock) but not yet 9 o'clock (or 12, 3, or 6 o'clock).

What Are Your Times?

Try to answer these questions. (You may need help figuring them out.)

What time do you usually wake up in the morning?

When do you eat lunch?

What time is school usually over?

When do you eat supper?

What time does your favorite TV show start? When is it over?

When is your bedtime?

What else do you usually do each day at about the same time? What times do you do these things?

> Use routines familiar to your child. If your child doesn't know the times that these routines usually occur, give the information. Then start referring to the clock often during the day whenever your child is doing these activities. While the actual times you do things may not be exact (except for TV programs), the experiences will help focus your child on making sense of what clocks and watches say.

Your Own Time Book

Make your own book of what times you do things on a school day. You can make a book by folding 2, 3, or more sheets of paper in half and fitting one inside the other.

On the front cover, write the title. Use *My Time Book* or anything else you'd like.

For each page, think of a time that you usually do something. Write the time or draw a picture of a clock showing that time. Draw a picture underneath of what you usually do at that time.

If you want to, write a sentence on each page that says:

At _____ o'clock, I _______________

_____________________________ .

The Timer Game

Here's a game that's good to try on a day when you are playing at home. You will need a kitchen timer or an alarm clock.

Start the game on the hour. Any hour is fine — 8 o'clock, 11 o'clock, 1 o'clock, or whatever. Ask someone to set the kitchen timer or the alarm clock for one hour later. What time do you think it will be in one hour?

Go back to what you were doing until you hear the timer or alarm go off. Then, look at a clock and see if you can tell what time it is. (You may need help doing this.) Talk about what you did in the last hour. Did the hour seem like a long time or a short time?

Reset the kitchen timer or alarm clock and wait for the next ring. What time do you think it will be then?

When the timer or the alarm rings, check a clock. Do this as many times as you can during the day.

On other days, if your child is comfortable telling the time on the hour, try the game with half-hour intervals. Begin at half past an hour and, with your child, read the time on a clock. Set the kitchen timer or alarm clock for half an hour, wait for the ring, and then read the time again. Tell your child that there are 30 minutes in half of an hour. It's probably too difficult for children to understand that 30 minutes is half of an hour, but introducing them to the information encourages children to think about it.

The Monster Math Game

The monsters play monster math at seven o'clock at night. You can play this game, too. You'll need a small paper bag and 6 to 8 buttons, beans, or pennies.

Start with just 5 objects in the bag. (Put the rest aside for later.) Reach into the bag, take out some of the objects, and show them to your partner. Your partner tells how many he or she thinks are left in the bag. Then dump out the bag and count the objects to make sure you have 5 altogether.

Take turns reaching into the bag so you both have chances to figure out how many are left in it. If you want, put in 6 or more objects to change the game.

Children develop number sense at different paces, and a game such as "Monster Math" will help. Play the game with your child as long as he or she is interested. Increase the number of objects, but if your child can only guess with a smaller number of objects, drop down to a lower number. Playing with fewer than 10 objects is appropriate for this age child.